Alfred Tennyson Tennyson

The Princess of Alfred Tennyson

Alfred Tennyson Tennyson

The Princess of Alfred Tennyson

ISBN/EAN: 9783337343330

Printed in Europe, USA, Canada, Australia, Japan

Cover: Foto ©Andreas Hilbeck / pixelio.de

More available books at **www.hansebooks.com**

THE PRINCESS

OF

ALFRED TENNYSON

RE-CAST AS A DRAMA

"Our Age is largely trying the experiment of the Princess."
TAINSH'S STUDY OF TENNYSON.

BOSTON
LEE AND SHEPARD, PUBLISHERS
NEW YORK
CHARLES T. DILLINGHAM
1881

Applications for permission to perform this Drama should be addressed to the Publishers.

Dedicated

TO THE LADIES AND GENTLEMEN

WHO APPEARED

IN A PRIVATE DRAMATIC PERFORMANCE

FOR WHICH

This Version of "The Princess"

WAS WRITTEN.

PREFACE.

"The Princess" is entitled "A Medley," being in form neither an epic nor a drama, though largely containing the elements of both. That its rich materials admit of more strictly dramatic treatment is suggested by the poet himself, in terms which might justify the attempt, if made in an appreciative spirit, with no purpose of disturbing the original, legitimate impression of the poem.

In this re-composition of the work, the aim has been to retain the language and style of Tennyson as far as possible, and only to take such liberties with the plot as have been experimentally found requisite in a private representation.

It is believed that a dramatic rendering of "The Princess," though it must necessarily sacrifice some of its literary beauties, can only enhance its charms as a wonderful creation of fancy, and may deepen its philosophical interest, as it bears upon many questions of modern social life and culture.

DRAMATIS PERSONÆ.

GAMA, Father of the Princess.

ARAC, }
TWIN BROTHERS, } Sons of Gama.

THE KING, Father of the Prince.

THE PRINCE, Lover of the Princess.

FLORIAN, }
CYRIL, } Friends of the Prince.

IDA, the Princess, and head of the College of Maidens.

BLANCHE, }
PSYCHE, } Ladies of the Court and Tutors in the College.

MELISSA, Daughter of Lady Blanche.

GIRL-STUDENTS. COLLEGE PORTRESS. WOMAN-POST. WOMAN-GUARDS. HERALDS.

ACT I.

SCENE I. — *A Presence-room in the* KING'S *Palace.*
SCENE II. — *Before* GAMA'S *Palace.*
SCENE III. — *A College-hall in the Palace of the* PRINCESS.

   I. *Interlude.* — "Sweet and low."

ACT II.

SCENE I. — *A Court of the* PRINCESS'S *Palace.*
SCENE II. — *A Park adjoining the Palace.*
SCENE III. — *On a Terrace before the Palace.*

  II. *Interlude.* — "The splendor falls on castle walls."

ACT III.

SCENE I. — *A Pavilion in the Park.*
SCENE II. — *On a Terrace before the Palace.*
SCENE III. — *A Council-Chamber in the Palace.*

 III. *Interlude.* — "Thy voice is heard through rolling drums."

ACT IV.

SCENE I. — *A Camp of the* KING'S *Army.*
SCENE II. — *Open Field between the Camps.*

  IV. *Interlude.* — "Home they brought her warrior dead."

ACT V.

SCENE I. — *A Hall of State in the* PRINCESS'S *Palace.*

  Finale. — "Ask me no more."

NOTE.

SOME of the longer passages, though well adapted for the closet, and even essential to the drama as read, may be omitted or curtailed in representation. — *See Bulwer's Note to "Richelieu."*

THE PRINCESS.

ACT I.

The King *seated, reading a letter, with an angry frown. A rich robe on the table before him. The* Prince *standing with* Cyril *and* Florian.

King (*tearing up the letter*).   An answer vague as wind !
    He takes our gifts :
Sends this return (*holding up the robe*) : grants that there
    did a kind
Of compact pass, a show of baby troth,
Betwixt his daughter and our son : he would
It might be kept to ; but she has a will
And maiden fancies ; loves to live alone
Among her women ; certain, will not wed.
Not wed !   I'll send a hundred thousand men
And bring her in a whirlwind.   (*Rends the robe in twain.*)
    Prince.   Let me go,
My father : some gross error surely lies
In this report, this answer of a king,
Whom all men rate as kind and hospitable.
    Florian.   I have a sister at the foreign court,
Who moves about the Princess ; she, you know,
Who wedded with a nobleman from thence ;
He, dying lately, left her, as I hear,

The lady of three castles in that land:
Through her this matter might be sifted clean.
    CYRIL.   And take me with you too : in those strange lands,
Trust me, I'll serve you better in a strait.
I grate on rusty hinges here.
    KING.   No ! no !
You shall not; 'tis our quarrel : we ourself
Will crush her pretty maiden fancies dead
In iron gauntlets : break the council up.   [*Exit* KING.
    FLORIAN.   One of her pretty fancies is, I hear,
A university for maidens ; she
The college head ; the tutors, Lady Blanche
And Lady Psyche, widows who had charge
Of her.   I've heard her sire, old Gama, say
They fed her theories, in and out of place,
Maintaining that with equal husbandry
The woman were an equal of the man,
And only knowledge makes the difference.
They harped on this, and praised her lofty odes
About the coming woman ; till at last
She begged of the good easy king to grant
To her a summer palace he had built
Hard by your father's frontier ; where she went
All wild to found a college like a man's.
    CYRIL.   'Tis said, they see no men ; but make it death
For any male thing but to peep at them.
They send a woman-post for all their news.
The land, I understand, for miles about
Is tilled by women, daughters of the plough ;
There is a plump-armed ostleress at the gate ;
The stable-boys are wenches —
    PRINCE.   Hist ! a thought
Has flashed, and must be clothed at once in act.

Remember how we three presented maid
Or nymph or goddess, at high tide of feast,
In masque or pageant at my father's court.
Send out and purchase female gear. Escaped
By night to Gama's palace ; there empowered
With letters which he cannot well refuse,
We pass approved the border sentries ; don
Our girl's attire betimes ; admitted, crave
The proper academic garb, whate'er
It be ; and so seek audience with the head,
The Princess, as arriving neophytes.
Once in that paradise, we test our fate.
Better such stratagem of love than war.

    CYRIL. Ha ! ha ! to see ourselves in such disguise
Would shake the midriff of despair itself
With laughter.

    FLORIAN. Who shall be our tutor there ?

    CYRIL. Who but the prettiest, the Lady Psyche ?

                                [*Exeunt.*

SCENE II.— BEFORE GAMA'S PALACE.

The towers of the imperial city in view. Enter KING GAMA *and*
    PRINCE ARAC *walking together and earnestly conversing.*

    GAMA. She will not see us ; not even you,
Nor me, nor her twin brothers, though we loved
And doted on her as a paragon.
'Twas all the fault of those two widows : they
Exiled our darling Ida from her home,
With talk of ladies' rights and woman's wrongs ;
Nothing but this : my very ears were hot
To hear them. Women, so they taught her, were

As children ; they must lose the child, assume
The woman : then, sir, awful odes she wrote
About this losing of the child, and rhymes
And dismal lyrics, prophesying change
Beyond all reason : these the women sang,
And called them masterpieces : — they mastered me.

  ARAC.   She flies too high, she flies too high !   And yet
She asked but space and fair play for her scheme :
She pressed and pressed it on me.   I myself,
What know I of these things? but, life and soul !
I thought her half right talking of her wrongs.
I say she flies too high ; 'sdeath, what of that?
If she but loved, — and, Sire, she can be sweet
To those she loves — I would the Prince might have her.

  GAMA.   With all my heart : so said I to our guest
Himself, when yestermorn, with his two friends,
He parted from me, urging at the last
Her plighted word and mine : what could I else
But own the claim, and give him letters to her?
Though, truth to tell, I rate his chance almost
At naked nothing.   [*Exeunt.*

SCENE III. — A COLLEGE-HALL OF THE PRINCESS.

*Statues, busts, scientific apparatus.   Forms for students.   A conspicuous
  inscription,* LET NO MAN ENTER HERE ON PAIN OF DEATH.   *The*
  PRINCESS *is discovered seated in state, with two leopards couched
  beside her throne, and tomes and papers at her feet : the* LADY
  BLANCHE *at the desk.   Enter* PORTRESS, *with paper, which* LADY
  BLANCHE *receives and reads.*

" Three ladies of the Northern empire pray
Your Highness would enroll them with your own
And Lady Psyche's pupils."

PRINCESS (*to* PORTRESS). Go and bid
Them hither. So begins the day to dawn [*Exit* PORTRESS.
Where last to look and least to hope for it.
Three converts from the scornful enemy!
    LADY BLANCHE. But why enrolled as Lady Psyche's
    pupils?
Must every novice, with crude choice, go sit
At her feet, learning only what before
Was taught in other rooms, half vacant now?
    PRINCESS. Be not so quick, dear Lady Blanche, to judge
These girlish preferences; but give them play,
And in due time, teacher or pupil, each
Shall find her like, and all a fitting meed
Of praise attain, as the good work moves on.
But here they come : receive them with due state.

(*Re-enter* PORTRESS *ushering the* PRINCE, CYRIL, *and* FLORIAN, *who
have assumed academic gowns of lilac and gold.*)

    PRINCESS (*rising*). We give you welcome : not without
    redound
Of use and glory to yourselves ye come,
The first-fruits of the stranger : aftertime,
And that full voice which circles round the grave,
Will rank you nobly, mingled up with me.
What! are the ladies of your land so tall?
    CYRIL. We of the court.
    PRINCESS. From the court? Then ye know the Prince !
    CYRIL. The climax of his age ! as though there were
One rose in all the world, your Highness that,
He worships only your ideal.
    PRINCESS. We scarcely thought in our own hall to hear
This barren verbiage, current among men,
Light coin, the tinsel clink of compliment.

Your flight from out your bookless wilds would seem
To argue love of knowledge and of power :
Your language proves you still the child.   Indeed,
We dream not of him.   When we set our hand
To this great work, we purposed with ourself
Never to wed.   You likewise will do well,
Ladies, in entering here, to cast and fling
The tricks, which make us toys of men, that so
You may, with those self-styled our lords, ally
Your fortunes, justlier balanced, scale with scale.
(*To* LADY BLANCHE.)   Let them now hear and sign their
          vows.

     LADY BLANCHE (*rising, reads from a large book*).   "Ye
          are
Not for three years to correspond with home ;
Not for three years to cross the liberties ;
Not for three years to speak with any men;
And all the college statutes ye will learn
And ever keep." — To this, your names.

          (*Kneeling, they write their names in the book.*)

     PRINCESS.   Now ye
Are green wood, see ye warp not.   Look, our hall !
Our statues ! not of those that men desire,
Sleek odalisques, or oracles of mode.
Nor stunted squaws of West or East ; but she
That taught the Sabine how to rule, and she
The foundress of the Babylonian wall,
The Carian Artemisia strong in war,
. The Rhodope that built the pyramid,
Clelia, Cornelia, with the Palmyrene
That fought Aurelian, and the Roman brows
Of Agrippina.   Dwell with these, and lose

Convention, since to look on noble forms
Makes noble through the sensuous organism
That which is higher. O lift your natures up :
Embrace our aims ; work out your freedom. Girls,
Knowledge is now no more a fountain sealed !
Drink deep, until the habits of the slave,
The sins of emptiness, gossip, and spite,
And slander die. Better not be at all
Than not be noble. But we go elsewhere.

(Rising, as the college bell rings.)

To-day the Lady Psyche will harangue
The fresh arrivals of the week before ;

(Enter PSYCHE *and train of girl students.)*

For they press in from all the provinces,
And fill the hive.

(Exeunt PRINCESS *and* LADY BLANCHE. STUDENTS *enter the forms,
and* LADY PSYCHE *goes to the desk and prepares to lecture.)*

FLORIAN *(aside)*. My sister !
CYRIL *(aside)*. Comely too, by all that's fair.
PRINCE *(aside)*. Oh, hush, hush !
LADY PSYCHE. This world was once a fluid haze of
      light,
Till toward the centre set the starry tides,
And eddied into suns, that wheeling cast
The planets : then the monster, then the man ;
Tattooed or woaded, winter-clad in skins,
Raw from the prime, and crushing down his mate ;
As yet we find in barbarous isles, and here
Among the lowest. (*Pauses.*)
      CYRIL *(aside)*. Lovely to the ear
As to the eye !

FLORIAN (*aside*).   My sister ever had
A wealth of graceful speech.
        PRINCE (*aside*).   A wealth of thought
Richer than speech.   But hist !
        LADY PSYCHE.   Long æons passed.
Then came the legendary Amazon,
As emblematic of a nobler age ;
And then the Persian, Grecian, Roman lines
Of empire with the woman's state in each
So far from just ; till Chivalry arose,
When some respect, however slight, was paid
To woman ; then commenced the dawn ;
A beam has slanted forward, falling in a land
Of promise ; fruit will follow.   Deep is now
Our debt of thanks to her who first has dared
To leap the rotten pales of prejudice,
Disyoke our necks from custom, and assert
None lordlier than ourselves but that which made
Woman and man.   She has founded : we must build.
Here may ye learn whatever men are taught :
Do not you fear ; some say your heads are less :
Some men's are small ; not they the least of men,
For often fineness compensates for size ;
Besides, the brain is like the hand, and grows
With using : thence the man's, if more, is more.
He took advantage of his strength to be
First in the field ; some ages have been lost :
But woman ripens earlier, and her life
Is longer ; and albeit our glorious names
Are fewer, scattered stars, yet since in truth
The highest is the measure of the man,
And not the Kaffir, Hottentot, Malay,
Nor those horn-handed breakers of the glebe,

But Homer, Plato, Verulam ; even so
With woman : and in arts of government,
Elizabeth and others ; arts of war,
The peasant Joan and others ; arts of grace,
Sappho and others vied with any man ;
And, last not least, she who has left her place,
And bowed her state to us, that we might grow
To use and power in this oasis, lapt
In the arms of leisure, sacred from the blight
Of ancient influence and scorn.

(*Concludes in a high oratorical strain.*)

O yet,

We trust, hereafter shall be everywhere
Two heads in council, two beside the hearth,
Two in the tangled business of the world,
Two in the liberal offices of life,
Two plummets dropt for one to sound the abyss
Of science, and the secrets of the mind ;
Musician, painter, sculptor, critic, more ;
And everywhere the broad and bounteous earth
Shall bear a double growth of those rare souls,
Poets, whose thoughts enrich the blood of the world.

(STUDENTS *applaud, and are dismissed.*)

LADY PSYCHE (*approaching and recognizing* FLORIAN).
My brother ! my brother !
FLORIAN.   Well, my sister.
LADY PSYCHE.   What do you here? and in this dress?
   and these?
Why, who are these? a wolf within the fold !
A pack of wolves ! the Lord be gracious to me !
A plot, a plot, a plot to ruin all !

FLORIAN.   No plot, no plot, my sister.
LADY PSYCHE.   Wretched boy,
How saw you not the inscription on the gate,
"LET NO MAN ENTER HERE ON PAIN OF DEATH"?
  FLORIAN.   And if I had beheld it, who would think
The softer Adams of your Academe,
O sister, sirens though they be, were such
As chanted on the blanching bones of men.
  LADY PSYCHE.   But you will find it otherwise.   You jest:
Ill jesting is it with edge-tools!   My vow
Binds me to speak, and oh! that iron will,
That axe-like edge unturnable, our Head,
The Princess.
  FLORIAN.   Well, then, Psyche, take my life,
And nail me like a weasel on a grange
For warning: bury me beside the gate,
And cut this epitaph above my bones,
"*Here lies a brother by a sister slain,*
All for the common good of womankind."
  CYRIL.   Let me die, too, having seen the Lady Psyche.
  PRINCE.   Albeit so masked, madam, I love the truth;
Receive it: and in me behold the Prince,
Your countryman, affianced years ago
To the Lady Ida: here, for here she was,
And thus (what other way was left?) I came.
  LADY PSYCHE.   O sir! O Prince! I have no country: mine,
If any, this; but none.   Whate'er I was
Disrooted, what I am is grafted here.
Affianced, sir? love-whispers may not breathe
Within this vestal limit; and how should I,
Who am not mine, say live? the thunderbolt
Hangs silent; but prepare: I speak; it falls.
  PRINCE.   Yet pause: for as to that inscription there,

I think no more of deadly lurks therein,
Than in a clapper clapping in a garth
To scare the fowl from fruit; if more there be,
If more and acted on, what follows? War;
Your own work marr'd ; for this your Academe,
Whichever side be victor, in the halloo
Will topple to the trumpet down, and pass
With all fair theories only made to gild
A stormless summer. (*Enter* MELISSA *unobserved.*)
 LADY PSYCHE. Let the Princess judge
Of that : farewell, sir — to you all, farewell.
I shudder at the sequel, but I go.
 PRINCE. Are you that Lady Psyche, — she that is
The fifth in line from that old Florian?
Yet hangs his portrait in my father's hall
(The gaunt old baron with his beetle brow
Sun-shaded in the heat of dusty fights)
As he bestrode my grandsire, when he fell
And all else fled ; we point to it, and we say,
The loyal warmth of Florian is not cold,
But branches current yet in kindred veins !
 FLORIAN. Are you that sister Psyche, she with whom
I sang and played about the morning hills,
Flung ball, flew kite, and raced the purple fly,
And snared the squirrel of the glen? are you
That Psyche, wont to bind my throbbing brow,
To smooth my pillow, mix the foaming draught
Of fever, tell me pleasant tales, and read
My sickness down to happy dreams? Are you
That brother-sister Psyche, both in one?
You were that Psyche, but what are you now?
 CYRIL. You are that lovely Psyche, she for whom
I would be that forever which I seem,

Woman, if I might sit beside your feet,
And glean your scattered sapience.
        PRINCE.   Are you
That Psyche, who, upon her bridal morn,
Before she parted from us, when the king
Kissed her pale cheek, declared that ancient ties
Would still be dear beyond the southern hills;
That, were there any of our people there
In want or peril, there was one to hear
And help them? look! for such are these and I.
        FLORIAN.   Are you that sister Psyche, she to whom
In gentler days, your arrow-wounded fawn
Came flying while you sat beside the well?
The creature laid his muzzle on your lap,
And sobbed, and you sobbed with it, and the blood
Was sprinkled on your kirtle, and you wept.
That was fawn's blood, not brother's, yet you wept.
You were that Psyche, but what are you now?
        LADY PSYCHE.   Out upon it! and why should I not play
The Spartan mother with emotion, be
The Lucius Junius Brutus of my kind?
Him you call great: and I, shall I, on whom
The secular emancipation turns
Of half this world, be swerved from right to save
A prince, a brother? a little will I yield.
Best so, perchance, for us, and well for you.
Oh hard, when love and duty clash! I fear
My conscience will not count me fleckless; yet —
Hear my conditions: promise (otherwise
You perish) as you came to slip away,
To-day, to-morrow, soon: it shall be said,
These women were too barbarous, would not learn;
They fled, who might have shamed us: promise, all.

PRINCE. What can we else? We promise, each and all.

LADY PSYCHE (*to* FLORIAN). I knew you at the first;
though you have grown,
You scarce have altered : I am sad and glad
To see you, Florian. *I* give thee to death,
My brother ! it was duty spake, not I.
My needful seeming harshness, pardon it.
Our mother, is she well?

MELISSA (*coming forward toward* LADY PSYCHE). I
brought a message here from Lady Blanche.

LADY PSYCHE. Ah — Melissa — you ! You heard us?

MELISSA. O pardon me !
I heard, I could not help it, did not wish :
But, dearest lady, pray you fear me not,
Nor think I bear that heart within my breast,
To give three gallant gentlemen to death.

LADY PSYCHE. I trust you, dear Melissa, for we two
Were always friends, none closer, elm and vine :
But yet your mother's jealous temperament —
Let not your prudence, dearest, drowse, or prove
The Danaïd of a leaky vase, for fear
This whole foundation ruin, and I lose
My honor, and these gentlemen their lives.

MELISSA. Ah, fear me not ! trust me, I would not tell,
No, not for all Aspasia's cleverness,
No, not to answer, madam, all those hard things
That Sheba came to ask of Solomon.

LADY PSYCHE. Be it so that we may lead the new light up.
And Solomon may come to Sheba yet.

CYRIL. But, madam, he the wisest man of men
Feasted the woman wisest then, in halls
Of Lebanonian cedar ; nor should you
Less welcome find among us, if you came

Among us, debtors for our lives to you,
Myself a debtor, too, for something more.

    LADY PSYCHE. Thanks, go; already we have been too
        long
Together: keep your hoods about your face;
They do so that affect abstraction here.
Speak little; all, I trust, may yet be well.

                    [*Exeunt* LADY PSYCHE *and* MELISSA.

    PRINCE (*surveying the room*). Why, sirs, they do all this
        as well as we.

    CYRIL. They hunt old trails, it may be, very well;
But when did woman ever yet invent?

    FLORIAN. Ungracious! can it be that you have learnt
No more from Psyche's lecture, you that talked
The trash that made me sick, and almost sad?

    CYRIL. O trash, indeed, but with a kernel in it.
Should I not call her wise who made me wise?
And learnt? I learnt more from her in a flash,
Than if my brain-pan were an empty hull,
And every Muse tumbled a science in.
A thousand hearts lie fallow in these halls,
And round these halls a thousand baby loves
Fly twanging headless arrows at the hearts,
Whence follows many a vacant pang.

    PRINCE.   It seems
With you, sir, entered in the bigger boy,
The Head of all the golden-shafted firm,
The long-limbed lad that had a Psyche too;
And cleft you through the stomacher.

    CYRIL.   And then
The doctors! O to hear the doctors! O
To watch the thirsty plants imbibing dews
Of knowledge!

FLORIAN. Yet you were as meek as any.

CYRIL. Ha! my zone unmanned me. Once or twice
I thought to roar and shake my mane ; but thou,
Modulate me, Soul of mincing mimicry !
Make liquid treble of that bassoon, my throat ;
Abase those eyes that ever loved to meet
Star-sisters answering under crescent brows ;
Abate the stride, which speaks of man, and loose
A flying charm of blushes o'er this cheek,
Where they like swallows coming out of time
Will wonder why they came : but hark, the bell (*bell rings*)
For vespers : let us go.   [*Exeunt.*

INTERLUDE I.

Sweet and low, sweet and low,
   Wind of the western sea,
Low, low, breathe and blow,
   Wind of the western sea !
Over the rolling waters go,
Come from the dying moon, and blow,
   Blow him again to me ;
While my little one, while my pretty one, sleeps.

Sleep and rest, sleep and rest,
   Father will come to thee soon ;
Rest, rest, on mother's breast,
   Father will come to thee soon ;
Father will come to his babe in the nest,
Silver sails all out of the west
   Under the silver moon :
Sleep, my little one, sleep, my pretty one, sleep.

24

ACT II.

SCENE I.—THE COURT OF THE PRINCESS'S PALACE.

*Columns, and urns of flowers. Statues of Muses and Graces. A foun-
tain. The* PRINCE, FLORIAN, *and* CYRIL *are viewing the sunrise.*

FLORIAN.   Now morn in the white wake of the morning
      star,
Comes furrowing all the orient into gold, —
Fit presage of our dawning, golden hopes !
   PRINCE.   Last night, as I read omens, Florian,
My dreams were not so golden as the dawn.
There lives an ancient legend in our house :   .
Some sorcerer, whom a far-off grandsire burnt
Because he cast no shadow, dying foretold
That none of all our blood should ever know
The shadow from the substance, and that one
Should come to fight with shadows, and to fall.
For so, my mother says, the story ran.
And, truly, waking dreams were more or less
An old and strange affection of the house.
Myself too have weird seizures, Heaven knows what !
Our great court-Galen calls them " catalepsy."
And last night, musing on the sorcerer's curse,
I saw contending armies in the land,
A camp hard by these gates, and mail-clad men
Trampling the flowers, and gleaming through the halls,
While tourney-lists were marshalled on the plain.
I seemed to move in old memorial tilts ;

25

And, doing battle with forgotten ghosts,
To dream myself the shadow of a dream,
When like a flash the weird affection came, —
Camp, college, army, turned to hollow shows,
And, gasping, I awoke in the broad day.

    CYRIL. Such fancies, Prince, are only bred of dreams
And shadows : bid them with the darkness flee.
The daylight cheerily calls us to our task :
I would that were as warlike as the dream.

(Enter MELISSA in terror, exclaiming.)

    MELISSA. Fly ! fly ! while yet you may ! My mother
      knows.
    PRINCE. How? Why?
    MELISSA (weeping). My fault, my fault ! and yet not mine :
Yet mine in part. O hear me, pardon me !
My mother, 'tis her wont from night to night
To rail at Lady Psyche and her side.
She says the Princess should have been the **Head**,
Herself and Lady Psyche the two arms :
And so it was agreed when first they came ;
But Lady Psyche was the right hand now,
And she the left, or not, or seldom, used ;
Her's more than half the students, all the love.
And so last night she fell to canvass you.

    FLORIAN. The countrywomen of the Lady Psyche?
    MELISSA. " *Her* countrywomen ! she did not envy her.
Who ever saw such wild barbarians ? "
    CYRIL. Why, we are very modest, proper girls.
    MELISSA. " Girls? more like men ! " and at these words
      the snake,
My secret, seemed to stir within my breast ;
And O sirs ! could I help it? but my cheek

Began to burn and burn, and her lynx eye
To fix and make me hotter, till she laughed :
" O marvellously modest maiden, you !
Men ! girls, like men ! why, if they had been men
You need not set your thoughts in rubric thus
For wholesale comment ! "

PRINCE.   You poor child ! and all
For our mad prank.

MELISSA.   Pardon ! I am shamed
That I must needs repeat for my excuse
What looks so little graceful.

CYRIL.   Rather blame
Our tell-tale shamelessness.

MELISSA.   " Men, men " (for still
My mother went revolving on the word),
" And so they are — very like men indeed —
And with that woman closeted for hours ! "
Then came these dreadful words out one by one,
" Why — these — *are* — men : " I shuddered : " and you
       know it ! "
O ask me nothing, I said.   " And she knows too,
And she conceals it ! "

PRINCE.   All is known, I fear,
And whelmed in failure.

MELISSA.   So my mother clutched
The truth at once, but with no word from me ;
And now thus early risen she goes to inform
The Princess : Lady Psyche will be crushed ;
But you may yet be saved, and therefore fly :
But heal me with your pardon ere you go.

CYRIL.   What pardon, sweet Melissa, for a blush ?
Pale one, blush again : than wear those lilies,
It were better to blush our lives away.

Yet let us breathe for one hour more in heaven,
Lest, hereafter, some classic angel speak
In scorn of us, "They mounted, Ganymedes,
To tumble, Vulcans, on the second morn."
But I will melt this marble into wax
To yield us further furlough.

      (MELISSA *shakes her head doubtingly.* *Exit* CYRIL.)

    FLORIAN.   But, tell us,
How grew this feud betwixt the right and left?
    MELISSA. O it was long ago : betwixt these two
Division smoulders hidden : 'tis my mother,
Too jealous, often fretful as the wind
Pent in a crevice ; much I bear with her.
I never knew my father, but she says
(God help her !) she was wedded to a fool.
And still she railed against the state of things.
She had the care of Lady Ida's youth,
And from the Queen's decease she brought her up.
But when your sister came she won the heart
Of Ida ; they were still together, grew
(For so they said themselves) inosculated ;
Consonant chords that shiver to one note :
One mind in all things : yet my mother still
Affirms your Psyche thieved her theories,
And angled with them for her pupils' love ;
She calls her plagiarist ; I know not what :
But I must go ; I dare not tarry here.
                             [*Exit* MELISSA.
    FLORIAN (*gazing after her*). An open-hearted maiden,
        true and pure.
If I could love, why, this were she. How pretty
Her blushing was, and how she blushed again,

As if to close with Cyril's random wish :
Not like your Princess, crammed with erring pride,
Nor like poor Psyche whom she drags in tow.

[*Exit* FLORIAN.

PRINCE (*soliloquizing*). Ah well ! the crane may chatter
    of the crane,
The dove may murmur of the dove, but I,
An eagle, clang an eagle to the sphere.
My Princess, O my Princess ! true she errs,
But in her own grand way. For her, and her,
Hebes are they to hand ambrosia, mix
The nectar ; but — ah, she — whene'er she moves
The Samian Herè rises, and she speaks,
A Memnon smitten with the morning sun.   [*Exit.*

SCENE II. — A PARK ADJOINING THE PALACE.

Enter PRINCESS, *pensively reading.*

PRINCESS.   Only a woman could have written thus.
(*Clasping the book to her breast.*)
Sweet songstress ! warbling from my native vale,
And from the distant, dear remembered past.

(*Reads.*)
" Come down, O maid, from yonder mountain height :
What pleasure lives in height, in height and cold ?
What pleasure in the splendor of the hills ?
But cease to move so near the heavens, and cease
To glide a sunbeam by the blasted pine,
To sit, a star, upon the sparkling spire :
And come, for Love is of the valley, come,
For Love is of the valley, come thou down
And find him."

A dream that once was mine ! Too late ! too late !

(*Closes the volume sadly, and walks on. Returning, meets the* PRINCE
entering, and they walk together.)

PRINCESS.　O friend ! we trust that you esteemed us not
Too harsh to your companion yestermorn ;
Unwillingly we spake.
　　　PRINCE.　　　　　　No — not to her,
But to another, one of whom we spake,
Your Highness might have seemed the thing you say.
　　　PRINCESS.　Again? are you ambassadresses sent
From him to me?　We give you, being strange,
A license : speak, and let the topic die.
　　　PRINCE (*at first stammeringly*).　Our king expects — was
　　　　　　there no pre-contract? —
There is no truer-hearted — ah, you seem
All he prefigured, and he could not see
The bird of passage flying south but longed
To follow : surely, if your Highness keep
Your purport, you will shock him even to death,
Or baser courses, children of despair.
　　　PRINCESS.　Poor boy, can he not read — no books?
Quoits, tennis, ball — no games? nor deals in that
Which men delight in, martial exercise?
To nurse a blind ideal like a girl,
Methinks he seems no better than a girl ;
As girls were once, as we ourself have been.
We had our dreams ; perhaps he mixt with them :
We touch on our dead self, nor shun to do it,
Being other — since we learnt our meaning here,
To lift the woman's fallen divinity,
Upon an even pedestal with man.

　　　　　　(*After a pause, more haughtily.*)

And as to pre-contracts, we move, my friend,
At no man's beck, but know ourself and him.
　　　PRINCE.　Alas, your Highness, I could wish you knew

Him better!—and then think how vast a work
To assail this gray pre-eminence of man!
Ere half be done perchance your life may fail;
Then comes the feebler heiress of your plan,
And takes and ruins all the work : and thus
With only Fame for spouse and your great deeds
For issue, you might live in vain, and miss,
Meanwhile, what every woman counts her due,
Love, home, and happiness.

    PRINCESS. Peace, you young savage of the Northern wild!
What! though your Prince's love were like a god's,
Have we not made ourself the sacrifice?
You are bold indeed : we are not talked to thus.
Yet will we say for children, would they grew
Like field-flowers everywhere! we like them well :
But children die ; and let me tell you, girl,
Howe'er you babble, great deeds cannot die ;
They with the sun and moon renew their light
Forever, blessing those that look on them.

    PRINCE (*aside*). Can this strange poet-princess with her
       grand
Imaginations e'er be won? I fear
'Tis but the wooing of a goddess, who   .
Will dazzle while she charms the hapless gaze.

    PRINCESS. No doubt we seem a kind of monster to you ;
We are used to that : for women up to this,
Cramped under worse than South-sea-isle taboo,
Have failed so far, they know not, cannot guess
How much their welfare is a passion to us.
O if our end were less achievable
By slow approaches, than by single act
Of immolation, any phase of death,
We were as prompt to spring against the pikes,

Or down the fiery gulf as talk of it,
To compass our dear sisters' liberties.   (*Feelingly.*)

(*They pause before a craggy bank, containing a mammoth fossil.*)

As these rude bones to us, are we to her
That will be.

PRINCE.   Dare we dream of that dread Power
Which wrought us, as the workman and his work
That only practice betters?

PRINCESS.   So we dream,
Who are but phantoms of succession, while
Creation is one act.   But how you love
The metaphysics ! read, and earn our prize,
A golden brooch : beneath an emerald plane
Sits Diotima, teaching him that died
Of hemlock ; our device ; wrought to the life ;
She rapt upon her subject, he on her :
For there are schools for all.

PRINCE.   And yet, methinks
I have not found one anatomic.

PRINCESS.   Nay,
We thought of that ; it pleased us not : in truth
We shudder but to dream our maids should ape
Those monstrous males that carve the living hound,
Or human frame ; and yet we know
Knowledge is knowledge, and this matter hangs.
Howbeit ourself, foreseeing casualty,
Unwilling men should come among us, learnt,
For many weary moons, before we came,
This craft of healing.   Were you sick,
Ourself would tend upon you.   So we work
Amid the fleeing shadows of the dawn,
And mould the woman of the fuller day.

(*They approach a flowery dell, with a lovely prospect beyond.*)

PRINCE.   How sweet to linger here with one that loved us !

PRINCESS.   Yea : rather say, with fair philosophies

That lift the fancy ; for indeed these fields

(*Moving toward the distant landscape.*)

Are lovely, — lovelier not the Elysian lawns

Where paced the demigods of old, and saw

The soft, white vapor streak the crownèd towers

Built to the sun.   [*Exit* PRINCESS.

(*The* PRINCE *stands gazing after the* PRINCESS.)

VOICE.   Follow !

PRINCE.   That voice — (*listening*).

VOICE.   Follow, thou shalt win.

PRINCE.   The same that rang through the wild woods at
       home,

Whither I went and looked for a still place,

And plucked her hidden likeness from my breast,

Laid it on flowers, and watched it lying bathed

In the green gleam of dewy-tasselled trees,

What time the whisp'ring south wind rose and swept
       the forest.

VOICE.   Follow !   Follow !   Follow !

(*The* PRINCE *disappears, the voice dying away.*)

SCENE III. — ON A TERRACE BEFORE THE PALACE.

Re-enter PRINCE, *looking abstracted and bewildered.* CYRIL, *having
entered, approaches yawning.*

CYRIL.   O hard task ! no fighting shadows here !

Better to clear prime forests, heave and thump

A league of street in summer solstice down,
Than hammer at this reverend gentlewoman.
    PRINCE.   And like a warrior you laid siege to her?
    CYRIL.   I knocked, and, bidden, entered, found her there
At point to move, and settled in her eyes
The green malignant light of coming storm.
    PRINCE.   I trust she did not seem to take offence.
    CYRIL.   Sir, I was courteous, every phrase well-oiled
As man's could be ; yet maiden-meek I prayed
Concealment : she demanded who we were,
And why we came. I fabled nothing fair,
But, your example pilot, told her all.
Up went the hushed amaze of hand and eye.
    PRINCE.   And when you dwelt upon our old affiance?
    CYRIL.   She answered sharply, that I talked astray.
    PRINCE.   Showed she no pity, fear, or policy?
    CYRIL.   I urged the fierce inscription on the gate,
And our three lives. True — we had limed ourselves
With open eyes, and we must take the chance.
But such extremes, I told her, well might harm
The woman's cause. " Not more than now," she said,
" So puddled as it is with favoritism."
    PRINCE.   And fair Melissa, said you naught of her?
    CYRIL.   I tried the mother's heart. Shame might befall
Melissa, knowing, saying not she knew.
Her answer was, " Leave me to deal with that."
    PRINCE.   What of the wrath of kings and public feuds?
    CYRIL.   I spoke of war to come and many deaths.
And she replied, her duty was to speak,
And duty, duty, clear of consequences.
    PRINCE.   You had indeed no easy argument.
    CYRIL.   I grew discouraged, sir ; but since I knew
No rock so hard but that a little wave

May beat admission in a thousand years,
I recommenced : " Decide not ere you pause.
I find you here but in the second place,
Some say the third — the authentic foundress you.
I offer boldly ; we will seat you highest :
Wink at our advent : help my Prince to gain
His rightful bride, and here I promise you
Some palace in our own land, where you shall reign
The head and heart of all our fair she-world,
And your great name flow on with broadening time
Forever."

PRINCE.　Ha ! the citadel must then
Have yielded.

CYRIL.　　Well, she balanced this a little,
And told me she would answer us to-day,
Meantime be mute ; thus much, no more, I gained.

(*Enter* MESSENGER.)

MESSENGER.　This afternoon the Princess rides to take
The dip of certain strata to the North.
You will go with her.　You shall find the land
Worth seeing ; and the river makes a fall
Out yonder.　There upon the sward
She bids her maids pitch her pavilion.　　　[*Exeunt.*

The splendor falls on castle walls
   And snowy summits old in story :
The long light shakes across the lakes,
   And the wild cataract leaps in glory.
Blow, bugle, blow, set the wild echoes flying,
Blow, bugle ; answer echoes, dying, dying, dying.

   O hark, O hear ! how thin and clear,
      And thinner, clearer, farther going !
   O sweet and far from cliff and scar
      The horns of Elfland faintly blowing !
Blow, let us hear the purple glens replying :
Blow, bugle ; answer, echoes, dying, dying, dying.

   O love ! they die in yon rich sky,
      They faint on hill or field or river :
   Our echoes roll from soul to soul,
      And grow forever and forever.
Blow, bugle, blow, set the wild echoes flying ;
And answer, echoes, answer, dying, dying, dying.

ACT III.

Sunset. Tripod bearing flowers, fruit, and incense. Enter Princess *and her train of students, with the* Prince, Cyril, *and* Florian.

PRINCESS.   There sinks the nebulous star men call the sun,
If that hypothesis of theirs be sound.
Let us down and rest.

(*They all sit down.*)

PRINCESS.   Let some one sing to us ;
Lightlier move the minutes fledged with music.
MAID (*sings*).

SONG.

Tears, idle tears, I know not what they mean,
Tears from the depth of some divine despair
Rise in the heart, and gather to the eyes,
In looking on the happy autumn fields,
And thinking of the days that are no more.

Fresh as the first beam glittering on a sail,
That brings our friends up from the underworld,
Sad as the last which reddens over one
That sinks with all we love below the verge ;
So sad, so fresh, the days that are no more.

Ah ! sad and strange as in dark summer dawns
The earliest pipe of half-awakened birds
To dying ears, when unto dying eyes
The casement slowly grows a glimmering square ;
So sad, so strange, the days that are no more.

37

Dear as remembered kisses after death,
And sweet as those by hopeless fancy feigned
On lips that are for others: deep as love,
Deep as first love, and wild with all regret;
O Death in Life! the days that are no more.

PRINCESS (*to* PRINCE). Know you no song of your own
    land,
Not such as moans about the retrospect,
But deals with the other distance and the hues
Of promise ; not a death's head at the wine?
    PRINCE (*sings*).

SONG.

O swallow, swallow, flying, flying South,
Fly to her, and fall upon her gilded eaves,
And tell her, tell her what I tell to thee.

O tell her, swallow, that thou knowest each,
That bright and fierce and fickle is the South,
And dark and true and tender is the North.

O swallow, swallow, if I could follow and light
Upon her lattice, I would pipe and trill
And cheep and twitter twenty million loves.

O were I thou that she might take me in,
And lay me on her bosom, and her heart
Would rock the snowy cradle till I died.

Why lingereth she to clothe her heart with love,
Delaying as the tender ash delays
To clothe herself, when all the woods are green?

O tell her, swallow, that thy brood is flown:
Say to her, I do but wanton in the South,
But in the North long since my nest is made.

O tell her, brief is life, but love is long,
And brief the sun of summer in the North,
And brief the moon of beauty in the South.

O swallow, flying from the golden woods,
Fly to her, and pipe and woo her, and make her mine,
And tell her, tell her, that I follow thee.

PRINCESS. A mere love-poem ! O for such, my friend,
We hold them slight : they mind us of the time
When we made bricks in Egypt.   Knaves are men
That lute and flute fantastic tenderness,
And play the slave to gain the tyranny.
Poor soul ! I had a maid of honor once ;
She wept her true eyes blind for such a one,
A rogue of canzonets and serenades.
I loved her. Peace be with her. She is dead.
Love is it? Would this same mock-love and this
Mock-Hymen were laid up like winter-bats,
Till all men grew to rate us at our worth,
Not vassals to be beat, nor pretty babes
To be dandled, no, but living wills, ensphered
Whole in ourselves, and owed to none.   Enough !
But now to leaven play with profit, you (*to* CYRIL),
Know you no song, the true growth of your soil,
That gives the manners of your countrywomen?
    CYRIL (*sings*).

SONG.

As I was walking down the street,
    Hi! ho! hi! ho! hi! ho!
A pretty girl I chanced to meet,
    Hi! ho! hi! ho! hi! ho!

PRINCESS.   Forbear !
PRINCE (*striking* CYRIL).   Forbear, sir !   (*A shriek from all.*)
MELISSA.   Flee the death !
PRINCESS.   To horse ! home ! to horse !
    (*All rush out in disorder, but* PRINCE, FLORIAN, CYRIL.)

A CRY OUTSIDE. The Head! the Head! the Princess!
O the Head!

(PRINCE, CYRIL, *and* FLORIAN *follow.*)

ANOTHER VOICE. She lives! She is saved!

SCENE II. — ON A TERRACE BEFORE THE PALACE.

Re-enter FLORIAN *and* PRINCE *meeting from opposite sides.*

FLORIAN. Who lives? and who is sav'd? The Princess?
PRINCE. Ay:
For blind with rage she missed the plank, and rolled
In the river. Out I sprang from glow to gloom:
There whirled her white robe like a blossomed branch
Rapt to the horrible fall: a glance I gave,
No more; but, woman-vested as I was,
Plunged; and the flood drew; yet I caught her; then
Oaring one arm, and bearing in my left
The weight of all the hopes of half the world,
Strove to buffet to land in vain. A tree
Was half-disrooted from his place, and stooped
Mid-channel. Right on this we drove and caught,
And grasping down the boughs I gained the shore.
There stood her maidens glimmeringly grouped
In the hollow bank. One reaching forward drew
My burthen from my arms; they cried, "She lives!"
And bore her to the palace: then alone,
With bee-like instinct hiveward, through the woods
I wandered hither. But how came you here?
FLORIAN. Last of the train, a moral leper, I,
To whom none spake, half-sick at heart, returned.
Arriving all confused among the rest
With hooded brows I crept, and heard unseen.

Girl after girl was called to trial : each
Disclaimed all knowledge of us : last of all,
Melissa ; trust me, sir, I pitied her.
She, questioned if she knew us men, at first
Was silent ; closer pressed, denied it not ;
And then, demanded if her mother knew,
Or Psyche, she affirmed not, or denied :
From whence the royal mind, familiar with her,
Easily gathered either guilt. She called
And sent for Psyche, but she was not there ;
She sent for Blanche to accuse her face to face ;
And I slipped out : but whither will you now?
And where are Psyche, — Cyril? Both are fled.
What, if together? that were not so well.
Would rather we had never come ! I dread
His wildness, and the chances of the dark.

 PRINCE. And yet you wrong him more than I that
  struck him.
The song might have been worse in grosser lips,
Beyond all pardon : for Cyril, howe'er
He deal in frolic, as to-night, I hold
'Twas but a flash upon the surface.

 FLORIAN.   Hist ! O hist !
They seek us : out so late is out of rules :
Moreover, "Seize the strangers !" is the cry.

(Enter PROCTORS, pursuing and seizing them.)

 PROCTORS. Names ! Names ! Come ye to the Princess.
[Exeunt.

SCENE III. — A COUNCIL-CHAMBER IN THE PALACE.

The PRINCESS *is discovered seated beneath a bright lamp.* WOMEN-GUARDS *behind her.* MAIDENS *on each side, combing out her hair, still damp from the river.* MELISSA *kneeling at her feet.* LADY BLANCHE *standing at a distance.*

PRINCESS.   O sisters, you have known what pangs we felt,
What heats of indignation, when we heard
Of those that iron-cramped their women's feet ;
Of lands in which at the altar the poor bride
Gives her harsh groom, for bridal gift, a scourge ;
Of living hearts that crack within the fire
Where smoulder their dead despots ; and I saw
That equal baseness lived in sleeker times
With smoother men : the old leaven leavened all :
Millions of throats would bawl for civil rights,
No woman named ; therefore I set my face
Against all men, and lived but for mine own :
Far off from men I built this fold for them :
I stored it full of rich memorial ;
I fenced it round with gallant institutes,
And biting laws, to scare the beasts of prey,
And prospered ; — till this rout of saucy boys
Brake on us at our books, and marred our peace,
Masked like our maids, blustering I know not what
Of insolence and love, some pretext held
Of old affiance — the striplings ! — for their sport ! —
I tamed my leopards : shall I not tame these ?
One poor lamb has but scarce escaped their wiles :

(Laying her hand on MELISSA'S *head.)*

What other victims may be, who can tell ?
And Psyche, where is she ?   I dread to think —

We seem a nest of traitors — none to trust.
But ere the budding treason grow to flower,
It shall be nipped in the arch-traitress here !

    (*Glances fiercely toward* LADY BLANCHE, *who comes forward.*)

    LADY BLANCHE.   It was not thus, O Princess ! in old days :
You prized my counsels, lived upon my lips :
I loved you like this kneeler, and you me,
Your second mother : those were gracious times.
Then came your new friend : you began to change —
I saw it and grieved — to slacken and to cool ;
Till, taken with her seeming openness,
You turned your warmer currents all to her,
To me you froze : this was my meed for all.
What student came but that you planed her path
To Lady Psyche, younger, not so wise,
I your old friend and tried, she new in all?
Yet I bore up in hope she would be known :

    (*Enter* PROCTORS *with* PRINCE *and* FLORIAN *as prisoners.*)

Then came these wolves : *they* knew her : *they* endured,
Long closeted with her the yestermorn,
To tell her what they were, and she to hear :
And me none told : not less to an eye like mine,
Last night, their mask was patent, and my foot
Was to you ; and again this very day
I came to tell you ; found that you had gone,
Ridden to the woods, she likewise : now, I thought.
That surely she will speak ; if not, then I.
Did she? these monsters blazoned what they were,
According to the coarseness of their kind,
For thus I hear ; and known at last,
And full of cowardice and guilty shame, she flies ;

And I remain, on whom to wreak your rage,
I, that have lent my life to build up yours,
I, that have wasted here health, wealth, and time
And talents, I — you know it — I will not boast:
Dismiss me, and I prophesy your plan,
Divorced from my experience, will be chaff
For every gust of chance, and men will say
We did not know the real light, but chased
The wisp that flickers where no foot can tread.
 PRINCESS (*coldly*). Your oath is broken: we dismiss
  you : go.
 LADY BLANCHE (*dragging up* MELISSA). The plan was
  mine. I built the nest, it seems,
To hatch the cuckoo. Rise ! and let us go.

   (*Enter* WOMAN-POST *in haste, with despatches.*)

 PRINCESS (*glancing through the letters angrily, and hand-
  ing the first to one of her* MAIDS). This from my
  father is of moment: read.
 MAID (*reads*). " Fair daughter, when we sent the Prince
  your way
We knew not your ungracious laws, which learnt,
We, conscious of what temper you are built,
Came all in haste to hinder wrong, but fell
Into his father's hands, who has this night,
You lying close upon his territory,
Slipped round and in the dark invested you,
And here he keeps me hostage for his son."
 PRINCESS (*tossing the other letter, and saying scornfully
  to the* PRINCE). And now, sir, we will hear your
  royal sire.
 MAID (*reads*). " You have our son : touch not a hair
  of his head.

Render him up unscathed; give him your hand:
Cleave to your contract; though indeed we hear
You hold the woman is the better man, —
A rampant heresy, which might well deserve
That we this night should pluck your palace down;
And we will do it, unless you send us back
Our son, on the instant, whole."

    PRINCE (*impetuously*). O not to pry and peer on your
      reserve,
But led by golden wishes, and a hope,
The child of regal compact, did I break
Your precinct; not a scorner of your sex
But venerator, zealous it should be
All that it might be. Let me say but this,
That many a famous man and woman, town
And landskip, have I heard of, after seen
The dwarfs of prestige; but in you I found
My boyish dream so dazzled down and so
O'er mastered, that, except you slay me here
According to your bitter statute-book,
I cannot cease to follow you, as they say
The seal does music; and howe'er you bar
Your heart with system out from mine, I hold
That it becomes no man to nurse despair,
But in the teeth of clenched antagonisms
To follow up the worthiest till he die:
Yet that I came not all unauthorized,
Behold your father's letter.

(*Kneeling, presents letter, which the* PRINCESS *seizes and dashes un-
opened at her feet. Hubbub outside, and crowd of girl-students enter.*)

    FIRST STUDENT. An army in the land!
    SECOND STUDENT.   Men! men within
The walls!

THIRD STUDENT. Ha! ha! What care we? Let them
 come.

(Confused shrieks and laughter from all.)

PRINCESS. What fear ye, brawlers? am not I your Head?
On me, me, me, the storm first breaks ; I dare
All these male thunderbolts : what is it ye fear?
Peace ! there are those to avenge us, and they come :
If not, — myself were like enough, O girls,
To unfurl the maiden banner of our rights,
And, clad in iron, burst the ranks of war,
Or, falling, protomartyr of our cause,
Die ! yet I blame ye not so much for fear ;
Six thousand years of fear have made ye that
From which I would redeem you : but for those
That stir this hubbub — you and you — I know
Your faces there in the crowd — to-morrow morn
We hold a great convention ; then shall they
Who love their voices more than duty, learn
With whom they deal, dismissed in shame to live
No wiser than their mothers, household stuff,
Live chattels, mincers of each other's fame,
Whose brains are in their hands and in their heels,
But fit to flaunt, to dress, to dance, to thrum,
Forever slaves at home and fools abroad.

(PRINCESS waves her hands, and crowd disperses.)

PRINCESS (*to* PRINCE). You have done well and like a
 gentleman,
And like a Prince ; you have our thanks for all :
And you look well too in your woman's dress :
Well have you done, and like a gentleman.
You saved our life ; we owe you bitter thanks :

Better have died and spilt our bones in the flood
Than men had said — but now — what hinders me
To take such bloody vengeance on you both? —
Yet since our father — Wasps in our good hive,
You would-be quenchers of the light to be,
Barbarians grosser than your native bears —
O would I had his sceptre for one hour !
You that have dared to break our bound and gulled
Our servants, wronged and lied and thwarted us —
I wed with thee ! *I* bound by precontract
Your bride, your bond-slave ! not though all the gold
That veins the world were packed to make your crown,
And every spoken tongue should lord you. Sir,
Your falsehood and yourself are hateful to us :
I trample on your offers and on you ;
Begone : we will not look upon you more.
Here, push them out at gates.

(They are ejected by women-guards.)

INTERLUDE III.

Thy voice is heard through rolling drums,
  That beat to battle where he stands;
Thy face across his fancy comes,
  And gives the battle to his hands:
A moment, while the trumpets blow,
  He sees his brood about thy knee;
The next, like fire he meets the foe,
  And strikes him dead for thine and thee.

ACT IV.

SCENE I.—A Camp of the King's Army.

Early dawn. A closed tent, guarded by CYRIL. *Camp-fires burning low. The* KING *lying on the ground asleep.*

(*Enter* PRINCE *and* FLORIAN *in bedraggled college gowns.*)

VOICE OF SENTRY. Stand ! Who goes?

PRINCE. Two from the palace.

VOICE. The second two ; pass on ! His Highness wakes.

KING (*laughing loud*). Ha ! ha ! ho ! ho ! our hostage
    king is free.
We did but keep him surety for our son,
If this be he, — or a draggled mawkin, thou,
That tends her bristled grunters in the sludge.

CYRIL (*whispering*). Look, he has been among his shad-
    ows, Sire.

KING. Satan take the old women and their shadows !
Now, make yourself a man to fight with men.
Go ! Cyril told us all.   [*Exit* KING.

CYRIL (*advancing*). Your pardon, Prince,
For my rude song.

PRINCE (*they shake hands*). And yours for my more rude
Retort ; let that pass : where is Psyche?

CYRIL. There in the tent ; and since she hither fled
Last night, she has not stirred nor spoken.

(*As* CYRIL *opens the tent,* LADY PSYCHE *is discovered lying prostrate
on the ground, wrapped in a soldier's cloak, a camp-woman watching
over her.*)

49

FLORIAN (*kneeling*).　　　　　　Come,
Lift up your head, sweet sister; lie not thus.
What have you done but right? You could not slay
Me, nor your prince : look up ; be comforted :
Sweet is it to have done the thing we ought,
When fallen in darker ways.

　　PRINCE. Be comforted : have I not lost her too,
In whose least act abides the nameless charm
That none has else for me?

　　PSYCHE. From her, my friend —
Parted from her — betrayed her cause and mine —
Where shall I breathe? Why kept ye not your faith?
O base and bad ! what comfort? none for me !

　　CYRIL. I pray thee, live, dear lady, for our sakes. [*Exit.*

SCENE II. — OPEN FIELD BETWEEN THE CAMPS.

Enter on one side, with a HERALD, *the* KING, CYRIL, *and* GAMA. *A parley sounded, and answered by another trumpet. Flourish. Enter on the other side, with a* HERALD, PRINCE ARAC *and his* TWIN BROTHERS.

　　KING (*to* GAMA, *who passes over to* ARAC'S *party*).
King, you are free, as by our royal word.
But look you, that our compact be fulfilled :
You have spoilt this child ; she laughs at you and man :
She wrongs herself, her sex, and me, and him.
But red-faced war has rods of steel and fire :
She yields, or war.

　　(*Enter the* PRINCE *and* FLORIAN *in armor, divested of college gowns.*)

　　GAMA (*to* PRINCE). We fear, indeed, you spent a stormy
　　　　time
With our strange girl : and yet they say that still

You love her.   Give us, then, your mind at large :
How say you, war, or not?

PRINCE.   Not war, if possible,
O King ! more soluble is this knot
By gentleness than war.   I want her love.
What were I nigher this, although we dashed
Your cities into shards with catapults?
She would not love ; and rather, Sire, than this,
I would the old god of war himself were dead.

   KING.   Tut ! tut ! you know them not, the girls.
Boy, when I hear you prate I almost think
That idiot legend credible.   Look you, sir,
There is no rose that's half so dear to them
As he that does the thing they dare not do,
Breathing and sounding beauteous battle, comes
With the air of the trumpet round him, and leaps in
Among the women, snares them by the score :
Thus I won your gentle mother, a good wife
Worth winning : but this firebrand — gentleness
To such as her ! if Cyril spake her true,
To catch a dragon in a cherry net,
To trip a tigress with a gossamer,
Were wisdom to it.

   PRINCE.   Yea, but hear me, Sire :
Wild natures need wise curbs.   The soldier?   No :
What dares not Ida do that she should prize
The soldier?   I beheld her, when she rose
The yesternight, and storming in extremes
Stood for her cause, and flung defiance down
Gage-like to man, and had not shunned the death,
No, not the soldier's : yet I hold her, King,
True woman : but you clash them all in one,
That have as many differences as we.

The violet varies from the lily as far
As oak from elm : one loves the soldier, one
The silken priest of peace, one this, one that,
And some unworthily ; but take them all in all,
Were we ourselves but half as good, as kind,
As truthful, much that Ida claims as right
Had ne'er been mooted, but as frankly theirs
As dues of Nature. To our point ; not war,
Lest I lose all.

GAMA.   Nay, nay, you speak but sense
And reason : we remember love ourselves
In our sweet youth ; we did not rate him then
This red-hot iron to be shaped with blows.
You talk almost like Ida : *she* can talk ;
But you talk kindlier : we esteem you for it. —
(*To the* KING.)   He seems a gracious and a gallant
      prince,
I would he had our daughter ; for the rest,
Our own detention, why, the causes weighed,
Fatherly fears — you used us courteously —
We would do much to gratify your prince —
We pardon it ; and for your ingress here
Upon the skirt and fringe of our fair land,
You did but come as goblins in the night,
Nor in the furrow broke the ploughman's head,
Nor robbed the farmer of his bowl of cream,
Nor bussed the milking-maid. But let your prince
Speak here with Arac ; Arac's word is thrice
As ours with Ida : something may be done —
I know not what — and ours shall see us friends.

ARAC.   Our land invaded, 'sdeath ! and he himself
Your captive, yet my father wills not war :
And, 'sdeath ! myself, what care I, war or no?

But then this question of your troth remains :
And there's a downright honest meaning in her.
I take her for the flower of womankind,
And so I often told her, right or wrong,
And, right or wrong, I care not : this is all :
I stand upon her side ; she made me swear it —
'Sdeath ! and with solemn rites by candle-light —
Swear by St. something — I forget her name —
Her that talked down the fifty wisest men ;
She was a princess too : and so I swore.

   (*Enter* WOMAN-POST *in haste with a letter, exclaiming.*)

WOMAN-POST.   The Princess to Prince Arac.
ARAC (*after glancing through the letter, reads*). "Whereas
   I know
Your prowess, Arac, and what mother's blood
You draw from, fight : you failing, I abide
What end soever ; fail you will not.   Still
Take not his life ; he risked it for my own :
His mother lives : yet whatsoe'er you do,
Fight and fight well ; strike, and strike home.   O dear
Brothers, the woman's angel guards you, you
The sole men to be mingled with our cause,
The sole men we shall prize in the after-time !
Farewell."
  KING (*aside*).   Stubborn ! but she may live to sit
Upon a king's right hand in thunder-storms,
And breed up warriors !   This spindling king,
This Gama swamped in lazy tolerance !
When the man wants weight, the woman takes it up,
And topples down the scales ; but this is fixt
As are the roots of earth and base of all :
Man for the field, and woman for the hearth ;

Man for the sword, and for the needle she ;
Man with the head, and woman with the heart ;
Man to command, and woman to obey ;
All else confusion.

    ARAC (*to the* PRINCE).   Come, this is all ; she will not :
      waive your claim.
If not, the foughten field, what else, at once
Decides it.   (*The* PRINCE *seems hesitating.*)

    FIRST BROTHER.   Ha ! no answer.   Like to like !
The woman's garment hid the woman's heart.

    CYRIL.   I'll answer for the Prince, nor I alone :
We cannot yield his claim, and will not.

    PRINCE.   Ay.
Decide it here : why not? we are three to three.

    SECOND BROTHER.   But three to three? no more than
      three to three ?
No more, and in our noble sister's cause?
More, more for honor ; every captain waits
Hungry for honor, angry for his King.
More, more, some fifty on a side, that each
May breathe himself, and quick ! by overthrow
Of these or those, the question settled, die.

    GAMA (*vainly expostulating*).   Boys ! boys !

    KING.   Ho ! ho !   Give but the chance, and we
Ourself would tilt it out among the lads.

    FLORIAN (*springing forward*).   Not fifty, but three hun-
      dred knights and more
Have sworn to combat for our claim till death.

    PRINCE.   Yea, and all, all for this wild wreath of air,
This flake of rainbow flying on the highest
Foam of men's deeds — this honor, if ye will, —
It needs must be for honor if at all :
Since what decision? if we fail, we fail ;

And if we win, we fail : she would not keep
Her compact.

ARAC.   'Sdeath ! we have her regal word
To bide this issue ; and the king's and mine.

KING.   To arms then ! and may Heaven defend the right.

[*Alarum.   Exeunt.*

Home they brought her warrior dead:
   She nor swooned, nor uttered cry.
All her maidens, watching, said,
   " She must weep, or she will die."

Then they praised him, soft and low,
   Called him worthy to be loved,
Truest friend and noblest foe ;
   Yet she neither spoke nor moved.

Stole a maiden from her place,
   Lightly to the warrior stept,
Took the face-cloth from the face;
   Yet she neither moved nor wept.

Rose a nurse of ninety years,
   Set his child upon her knee —
Like summer tempest came her tears —
   " Sweet my child, I live for thee."

ACT V.

The PRINCESS enthroned, attended by her maidens and LADY
BLANCHE and MELISSA.

PRINCESS.   Our enemies have fallen, have fallen : the
    seed,
The little seed they laughed at in the dark,
Has risen and cleft the soil, and grown a bulk
Of spanless girth, that lays on every side
A thousand arms, and rushes to the sun.
Our enemies have fallen, have fallen : they came ;
The leaves were wet with women's tears : they heard
A noise of songs they would not understand :
They marked it with the red cross to the fall,
And would have strown it, and are fallen themselves.
And now, O maids, behold our sanctuary
Is violate, our laws broken : fear we not
To break them more in their behoof, whose arms
Championed and won our cause.   Come, then,
We will be liberal, since our rights are gained.
Let them not lie in the tents with coarse mankind,
Ill nurses ; but descend and proffer these,
The brethren of our blood and cause, that there
Lie bruised and maimed, the tender ministries
Of female hands and hospitality.
        (*Trumpet.   Enter* HERALD *of* PRINCE ARAC.)

HERALD. Tidings, your Highness, from the glorious field!
The prince has fallen wounded in the fray,
And dies, or only lives your prisoner.
These trinkets from his neck Prince Arac sends
As trophies.

(*Kneels, and presents to* PRINCESS *a miniature, and tress of hair.*)

PRINCESS. Alas! alas! my likeness! and the tress
My mother shore with kisses on the day —
The day I was betrothed to the Prince.

(*Enter* GAMA, ARAC, *the* KING, CYRIL, *and* PSYCHE *in her riding-habit.*)

He saved my life : my brother slays him for it.
(*To the* KING.) O sire! O let me have him! if he lives —
Here in the palace : we will tend on him
With our own hands ; if so, by any means,
To lighten the great clog of thanks, that makes
Our progress falter to the woman's goal.
THE KING. Madam, the Prince still lives, it may be
    maimed,
But not yet hurt to death for your wild whim.
PSYCHE (*kneeling to the* PRINCESS). We two were friends :
    I go to mine own land
Forever ; find some other : as for me,
I scarce am fit for your great plans : yet speak to me,
Say one soft word, and let me part forgiven.

(*The* PRINCESS *is silent.*)

ARAC. Out upon you, Ida! you blame the man :
You wrong yourselves — the woman is so hard
Upon the woman. Come, a grace to me!
I am your warrior ; I and mine have fought

Your battle : kiss her, take her hand, she weeps.
'Sdeath ! I would sooner fight thrice o'er than see it.

(*The* PRINCESS *is still abstracted.*)

GAMA.   I've heard that there is iron in the blood,
And I believe it.   Not one word?   Not one?
Whence drew you this steel temper?   Not from me,
Not from your mother, now a saint with saints.
She said you had a heart — I heard her say it —
" Our Ida has a heart," — just ere she died —
" But see that some one with authority
Be near her still," and I — I sought for one —
All people said she had authority —
The Lady Blanche : much profit !
    KING.   O you,
Woman, whom we thought woman even now,
And were half fooled to let you tend our son,
Because he might have wished it — but we see
The accomplice of your madness unforgiven,
And think that you might mix his draught with death,
When your skies change again : the rougher hand
Is safer for the Prince ; back to the tents ! — (*Turns as if
    to go.*)
    PRINCESS.   Come hither, Psyche, and embrace me, come
Quick, while I melt ; make reconcilement sure
With one that cannot keep her mind an hour :
Come to the hollow heart they slander so !
Kiss and be friends, like children being chid !
I seem no more : I want forgiveness too :
I should have had to do with none but maids,
That have no links with men.   Ah false but dear,
Dear traitor, too much loved ! why? — why?   Yet see,
Before these kings we embrace you yet once more

With all forgiveness, all oblivion,
And trust, not love, you less.   (*They embrace.*)
(*To the* KING.)   And now, O sire,
Grant me your son, to nurse, to wait upon him
Like mine own brother.   For my debt to him,
This night-mare weight of gratitude, taunt me not.
Help, father, brother, help ! speak to the king.
Thaw this male nature to some touch of that
Which kills me with myself, and drags me down
From my fixed height to mob me up with all
The soft and milky rabble of womankind,
Poor weakling even as they are.   (*Weeps.*)
  CYRIL (*to* PSYCHE).   Your brother, Lady — Florian, — ask
   for him
Of your great Head — for he is wounded too —
That you may tend him with the Prince.
  PRINCESS.   Ay so,
Our laws are broken, let him enter too.
  MELISSA (*kneeling to* PRINCESS).   Let me too wait with
   her on Florian.
  CYRIL.   And Violet, whose tearful song made such
Sweet prelude to my rougher music, has
A cousin tumbled on the plain.   For him
We urge the same petition.   (*He kneels to the* PRINCESS.)
  PRINCESS.   Ay so,
I stagger in the stream ; I cannot keep
My heart an eddy from the brawling hour.
We break our laws with ease, but let it be. [*Exit* CYRIL.
  BLANCHE.   Ay so?   Amazed indeed am I to hear
Your Highness : but your Highness breaks with ease
The law your Highness did not make ; 'twas I.
I had been wedded wife ; I knew mankind,
And blocked them out ; but these men came to woo
Your Highness — verily, I think to win.

Princess. Fling our doors wide ! All, all, not one, but all.
Not only he, but, by my mother's soul,
Whatever man lies wounded, friend or foe,
Shall enter, if he will.   Let our girls flit
Till the storm die !   She fain would sting us too,
But shall not.   Pass, and mingle with your likes.
We brook no further insult.

(Flourish.   Enter HERALD, CYRIL, FLORIAN, *and the* PRINCE.)

Herald.   The Prince ! the Prince ! not wounded, but
    alive   .
And whole ; for stunned and fallen in a swoon
He lay among his enemies, despoiled
And left for dead, but waked among his friends,
And found that real which he thought a dream.
    Cyril.   No more to fight with shadows and to fall,
He comes to claim henceforth the substance.
    The King.   And so you have our son, most gracious
        Queen,
As you desired.
    Gama.   And you, our daughter, Prince,
By right of pre-contract, or as you like.
    Princess.   Thus all my labor is but as a block
Left in the quarry ; fruitless my war
Against the sons of men and barbarous laws,
Waged less for truth in knowledge than for power :
And I have failed in sweet humility — failed in all.
Ah fool, that made myself a Queen of Farce !
When comes another such ? never, I think,
Till the sun drop dead from the signs.

(The PRINCESS *bows her head upon her hands.)*

Prince.   Blame not thyself too much, O Queen ! nor
    blame

Too much the sons of men and barbarous laws;
These were the rough ways of the world till now.
Henceforth thou hast a helper, me, that know
The woman's cause is man's; they rise or sink
Together, dwarfed or godlike, bond or free :
For woman is not undevelopt man,
But diverse; could we make her as the man,
Sweet love were slain : his dearest bond is this,
Not like to like, but like in difference.
Yet in the long years liker must they grow;
The man be more of woman, she of man;
He gain in sweetness and in moral height,
Nor lose the wrestling thews that throw the world;
She mental breadth, nor fail in household care,
Nor lose the childlike in the larger mind;
Till at the last she set herself to man,
Like perfect music unto noble words.
Then comes the statelier Eden back to men;
Then reign the world's great bridals, chaste and calm;
Then springs the crowning race of humankind.
May these things be !

(*The* PRINCESS *rising, is handed down by the* PRINCE; CYRIL *joining*
PSYCHE, *and* MELISSA *joined by* FLORIAN.)

PRINCE.   Oh, we will walk this world,
Yoked in all exercise of noble end !
And so through those dark gates across the wild
That no man knows.

FINALE.

Ask me no more : the moon may draw the sea ;
　The cloud may stoop from heaven and take the shape,
　With fold to fold, of mountain or of cape ;
But O too fond! when have I answered thee ?
　　　　Ask me no more.

Ask me no more : what answer should I give ?
　I love not hollow cheek or faded eye :
　Yet, O my friend ! I will not have thee die.
Ask me no more, lest I should bid thee live ;
　　　　Ask me no more.

Ask me no more : thy fate and mine are sealed :
　I strove against the stream, and all in vain :
　Let the great river take me to the main :
No more, dear love, for at a touch I yield ;
　　　　Ask me no more.

www.ingramcontent.com/pod-product-compliance
Lightning Source LLC
Chambersburg PA
CBHW031248260626
47169CB00007B/2495